Sisters wit

Hearts

Sisters with Glass
Hearts

and other classic fairy-tales

Retold by Fiona Waters

Illustrated by
Gail Newey

BLOOMSBURY
CHILDREN'S
BOOKS

For Venetia, with love

First published in Great Britain in 2000
Bloomsbury Publishing Plc, 38 Soho Square, London, W1V 5DF

Copyright © Text Fiona Waters 2000
Copyright © Illustrations Gail Newey 2000

The moral right of the author has been asserted
A CIP catalogue record of this book is available from the
British Library

ISBN 0 7475 4709 2

Printed in England by Clays Ltd, St Ives plc

10 9 8 7 6 5 4 3 2 1

Contents

The Three Sisters and Their Glass Hearts

A story from goodness knows where

Once upon a time there lived a King and Queen and their three lovely daughters. And they would have all been very happy but for the great misfortune that the three girls had been born with glass hearts. They were not allowed to

play with any of the other children
in the palace, and they had to sleep
in huge beds piled high with
cushions in case they tossed and
turned too much while asleep. But
all the precautions in the world
could not protect them for ever.

One day the eldest girl was looking out of the window at the palace gardens when she caught sight of the most brilliantly coloured butterfly. She leaned out further to get a better look when suddenly there was the most dreadful sound

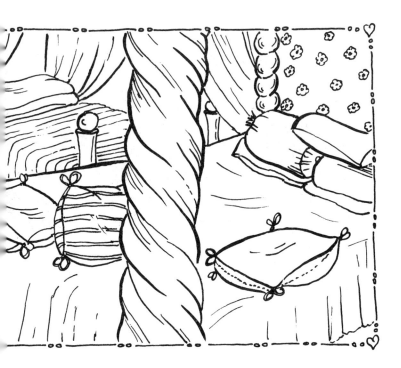

of breaking glass! The poor Princess had broken her heart.

The whole palace was in mourning for weeks. The other two sisters were wrapped up even more carefully and their lives were really very dull. The Queen was worn to a ravelling as she fussed and fidgeted around them and the King became very gloomy for he could see the girls growing paler and sadder as the months went by. And alas! all their precautions were in vain. In a thoughtless moment the second Princess drank a very hot cup of coffee. There was a loud crack, and the Princess felt a sharp

pain in her chest. All the court physicians, advisors and chamberlains ran around in a huge flap and fuss, wringing their hands and bewailing the fate of the royal family. Fortunately for the Princess, she had a very sensible little

chambermaid who cleared all the
courtiers out of the room and shut
the doors very firmly. To the great
relief of the King and Queen, the
Princess had only cracked her heart
and was still very much alive.

The third sister grew up and

became very beautiful. Because she
had to spend so much time sitting
quietly reading books she was also
very clever and it was not long

before many wealthy and handsome princes came from far off lands seeking her hand in marriage. The King looked at them all askance.

'I will only give my beloved daughter in marriage if her suitor is high born, very wealthy and also a glazier able to mend her poor heart if she should meet with an accident.'

Well, needless to say, not one of the rich princes or wealthy noblemen had the slightest idea about how to rivet broken glass so all their vows of undying love were in vain and they returned sadly to their native lands with only their memories of the beautiful and clever Princess as a consolation.

The Princess was getting very bored with all the dull young men who were presented to her as potential husbands.

Now there was in the royal

palace a young page whose duty it
was to carry the youngest
Princess's train on ceremonial
occasions. He took this duty very
seriously, so much so that the
Princess noticed how good he was
and always made a point of
thanking him specially. This made

the young man blush and quite unsettled him for he had long loved the Princess from afar. One day the selection of princes had been particularly awful and as the Princess swept from the throne room she turned to her faithful page and said,

'Oh, why are you not a prince and a glazier? You are so much nicer than all these dreadful weak kneed and dreary princes I have to suffer!'

The young page blushed hugely at her words, feeling very confused, and having retreated from the Princess with a deep and

polite bow, he rushed into the
courtyard to plunge his flaming
cheeks into the fountain. As he sat
by the splashing water he had a
sudden and very bold thought.

Without pausing to think any
further in case he lost his resolve,
he strode off into the town and
sought out a glazier.

'I would like you to teach me to

become a glazier,' he said to the
astonished man.

'I can certainly teach you, but it will take three years.'

The page was horrified and asked if there was no way he could achieve his ambition faster.

'Not if you want to be a proper glazier,' replied the man. 'That is how long it took me, and my father before me.'

So the page resigned himself to his fate and was apprenticed to the glazier. At first he was only allowed to sweep the workshop floor and run messages for the busy glazier. But as we know he was a conscientious young man and the glazier soon trusted him to help in the cutting of the glass. Then he progressed to putting in putty to stop up the cracks in the palace windows. This pleased the young man as it meant he could catch occasional glimpses of his former mistress, the youngest Princess. He thought she looked pale and sad, and he certainly did not think her new page made a very good job of carrying her train.

Slowly, slowly the years passed as the glazier taught the young man all he knew, until the day came when he said,

'There is no more I can teach you, young man. Truth to tell, I think

you are a better glazier than I am. I
wish you well.'

The young man, who had grown
tall and strong in the three years he
had been away from the palace,
went and bought himself a fine

new suit of green velvet with lace
ruffles at the cuffs and neck. He
went to the stables and hired a
magnificent white horse with a
flowing mane, and finally, bought a
singing linnet in a golden cage.

Then he set off for the palace. On the way there he met a great crowd of people, all jostling and pushing.

'What is happening?' he asked an elderly man, resting by the side of the road.

'Our King has just issued a decree that as he has failed to find a prince who is a glazier to marry his youngest daughter, he will consider anyone who is a glazier as long as he shall please the Princess,' said the old man.

You can imagine how much this encouraged our young man and he urged his horse on into the palace gates. The courtyard was thronged

with would be suitors and the poor
Princess had a headache. Through
all the hubbub she heard the sweet
twitterings of the linnet in the
golden cage and she asked one of
the courtiers to find the little bird
and bring it to her. Naturally the

young man insisted on carrying the
cage himself, and when he reached
the Princess he bowed very low at
her feet and said,

'Princess, do you remember your
page who used to carry your train
so well?' and as he lifted his head

the Princess recognised him.

'Oh, where have you been?' she cried. 'I have missed you so much!' and then she blushed furiously.

'I have been apprenticed to a glazier for three years and am now able to look after you properly. Will you marry me?' asked the young man all in a great rush.

Then he blushed furiously too.

The King and Queen were delighted at this turn of events and in no time at all the wedding was arranged. The young man took very great care of his Princess and she never had any cause to need her husband's hard won skills as a

glazier. They had lots and lots of children, all of whom I am glad to say had perfectly normal hearts. The Princess insisted that the little linnet be given her freedom from the golden cage as long as she

would return once a year to sing to
them so they would never forget
how they were brought together
again. They all lived very happily
ever after including the second
Princess, the one with the cracked

heart, who was an excellent aunt to all the little princesses and princes.

Sister of Bones

A story from East Africa

Once in the dusty plains of Africa there was a family who had two daughters, Chido and Njoki. The girls had to work very hard as there was a great deal to be done every day. First thing in the morning they had to cook breakfast

and then they had to collect water
from the river. Then they had to
sweep the yard, grind the maize
and help look after all the children
in the village.

The hardest task was collecting

the water. In the rainy season there
was plenty of clean and sparkling
water to be had from a nearby well,
but when it was dry the water had
to come from the river which was a
long way off. It would take a whole

morning to collect and the hollowed out gourds the water was carried in became heavier and heavier with every step. The sun was high in the sky and burning hot, and the dry wind would fill the girls' eyes with dust. Lizards would scuttle off into the bush as their feet shuffled along the track, and the gaily coloured birds would squawk their displeasure at being disturbed.

Chido would do most of the carrying. Njoki was not able to manage the great heavy gourds, her arms were thin and her legs became tired when she walked for

any distance. Usually she stayed at
home and plucked the chickens for
supper or sang to the other
children for she had a sweet voice.
Her parents had taken her to the
witch doctor to find out why she
was so thin and weak but all his

potions and spells had failed to
improve her condition. Njoki was
sad that she was not as strong as
her sister but she never
complained. There was still plenty
of work for her to do in the village.

Chido always filled the water

gourds at the same place on the
river bank. There was a path
leading down to the water which
had been made over time by the

animals coming to drink at a deep pool. She liked to look at their footprints and see which beasts had been there before her. She could tell when the leopard had been there at night and when the shy little antelopes had come down to drink on their spindly legs just as the sun was rising. She would scoop up a few handfuls of water for herself and rest before she set off on the long, hot journey home.

One dreadful day as she was leaning over the pool to take a drink, she slipped on the muddy bank and fell headfirst into the river. Chido could not swim and

the pool was very deep. She
struggled desperately to reach the
river bank but the current pulled
her down and with one last cry she
sank beneath the surface. The
monkeys in the trees chattered in

fright and bounded away, and soon the pool was still again.

Back in the village the afternoon slipped by and when Chido had not returned by sunset her family knew that something had

happened to her. They did not dare to venture out at night because of all the wild animals roaming round the village but at first light her father and all the village men set off in search of her. They ran all the way to the river bank and there they saw her footprints leading down to the river's edge. They also saw to their great distress that there were no footprints coming back up the bank and it was all too obvious what had happened to poor Chido.

There was great sadness in the village that night for everyone had loved Chido as she had always

done her work cheerfully and was
full of fun and laughter. Njoki sat
alone in the hut they had shared
and cried bitterly. She felt
somehow to blame as she had
never been able to help her sister

carry the heavy gourds. She
realised that from now on she
would have to fetch the water as
there was no one else who could be
spared.

The next morning before the sun

had risen, Njoki set off with a
heavy heart but determined to
carry the water back to the village.
It took her all day, and she had to

stop many, many times to rest and when she lay down that night in her lonely hut she felt she would never be able to stand up again, far less walk. But somehow the next morning she managed and again the next morning and the next. And so she struggled for many days and it never seemed to become any easier.

One day as she sat resting on the same bank where her sister had disappeared, Njoki began to sing a song all about how her sister had drowned and how much she missed her. It was a very sad song and as Njoki's lovely voice reached

across the deep pool many animals
crept closer to her to listen. The
crocodiles slid into the water to get
closer and even they felt sorry for
her as they listened to her words.
When Njoki finished singing they

all dived deep into the pool with a
great splash which frightened her.
She stood up in a hurry, ready to
start the long trek back to the
village with the heavy gourds. But
as she turned to go, there was

another great splash from the river as the crocodiles appeared again, carrying a bundle of bones in their great teeth. They laid the bones at Njoki's feet and to her great astonishment and even greater joy Chido was standing before her fully restored to life. They hugged and kissed each other and laughed and cried and then hugged and kissed all over again.

'Come sister, let me carry the gourds for you. I am stronger,' said Chido as she strode up the river bank. And she carried the water all the way to the edge of the village where she stopped and said,

'You must carry the water into the village as I must now return to the crocodiles. They want me to stay with them in the river.'

And she hugged Njoki and

turned back towards the river.

From that day on, whenever Njoki reached the river bank, Chido would be waiting for her and together they would fill the gourds. As they walked back to the village, Chido would sing and

laugh and tell Njoki all about life in the river with the crocodiles.

It was too big a secret for Njoki to keep, and one day she told her parents that their elder daughter was alive and helped her to carry the water every day. Needless to

say her parents did not believe her at first and were very angry, but Njoki managed to persuade them to accompany her to the river and there they saw with their own eyes that their beloved Chido was indeed alive. To thank the crocodiles, the father and all the men in the village went out hunting and laid great piles of meat on a rock by the river. The crocodiles quickly smelt the meat and gobbled it up with their great big teeth and then slid back into the water. The crocodiles released Chido from her life in the river on the understanding that the men in

the village would provide them with meat on a regular basis. And from that point on, the spring never ran dry so Chido and Njoki didn't have to walk all the way to the river in the heat of the day to fetch water for the village.

The Three Sisters Who Were Trapped in a Mountain

A story from Norway

A long, long time ago there lived a poor old widow under a mountain, way in the back of beyond. She had three daughters and their only possession was a hen. Needless to say, this hen was the most spoiled and cosseted creature in the world.

The old woman would keep the hen on her knee and stroke and pet it all day long. And so they existed from day to day.

But one dark day the hen disappeared. They searched high and low inside their humble cottage, and then scoured the bleak and barren landscape outside, but the hen was nowhere to be seen. At last the old woman called the eldest sister and said,

'You must go and look for our hen, we cannot survive without her.'

So the eldest sister set off, calling all the while to the hen. She walked

and walked all day until she was
right up against the foot of the
mountain and had just decided to
rest for a while when she fell
down, down deep into the earth
under the mountain. She landed
with a great bump on a pile of

leaves. Once she had drawn breath
she looked round and found
herself in a huge vaulted room,
richly furnished with velvet
curtains, deep silky carpets and
fine carved chairs. She set off to
explore, and was wandering from

room to room, each more beautiful
than the one before, when
suddenly she was confronted by a
huge ugly troll.

'Ah hah!' says he. 'Will you be
my wife?'

'Certainly not,' says she for the
troll was very ugly indeed and
anyway she didn't wish to spend
the rest of her days living deep
under the earth.

Well, trolls don't usually take no
for an answer, so he chopped off
her head ere she could blink and
threw her body into his cellar.

In the meantime, the mother and
the two other sisters sat at home

waiting and waiting and waiting.
After a long time, the mother said
to the middle sister,

'You must go and look for the

hen, and perhaps you will find
your sister on your journey.'

So the middle sister set off,
following in her sister's footsteps.
And she too fell down the hole
deep, deep into the mountain and
eventually met the troll who asked

her to marry him, just as before.
She was no more enamoured with
him than her sister had been and
also refused. The troll chopped off
her head ere she could blink and
flung her into the cellar alongside
her sister.

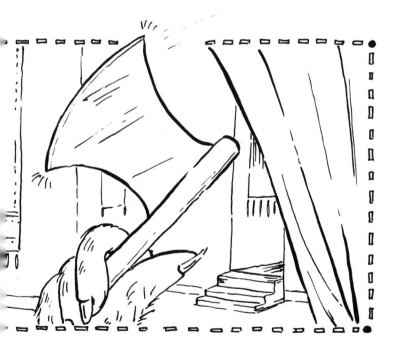

So the mother and her youngest daughter waited and waited and waited for the middle daughter to return and after a long time the mother said to the youngest daughter,

'You must go and look for the hen and perhaps you will find your sisters on your journey.'

Now the youngest daughter was as sharp as a new knife so she kept her wits about her as she searched the land under the mountain. When she reached the foot of the mountain she knew at once that there was some mischief afoot. She spotted the hole opening up before

her feet and saw steps cut deep
into the side of the rock going
down into the earth under the
mountain. She climbed down very
carefully until she reached the
bottom. Then she looked around
the lavish rooms. She found the

cellar and saw the bodies of her
two sisters lying there but she
remained calm and alert. So when
the troll bounded into the room she
was able to greet him with a smile.

'Will you marry me?' he asked
without any preamble.

'Certainly,' she said, for she saw

how her sisters had fared.

The troll was delighted and brought her many rich clothes and jewels and splendid shoes, and began to make elaborate preparations for their wedding, until one day he came into her chamber and found her in tears.

'Why are you crying? Have I not given you everything you could wish for and more?' he said.

'Oh yes,' she replied, 'but I do wish to tell my mother about our marriage. She will be anxious that I have been gone so long.'

The troll promised he would let her send a message to her mother with a bag of food. The clever girl filled a sack with gold and silver and then put some food on top. The troll thought the sack was very heavy but he wasn't very bright and didn't think to look inside as he dumped it on the old widow's doorstep that night. When the

widow saw the food she was
delighted, but when she saw the
gold and silver she became very
thoughtful.

'My sharp youngest daughter has

something to do with this, I'll be bound,' she said, and she felt more cheerful than she had done for some time.

The troll set off home again without a glance to left or right. You know, of course, that trolls can

only come out at night, for just a
single ray of sunshine will turn
them to stone on the spot. He
reached the steps cut deep into the
side of the rock and as he raced
down them, a little mountain goat
tumbled down with him.

'Who asked you to accompany me?' he roared and chopped off the goat's head ere it could blink.

'Why did you do that?' the youngest sister cried. 'I would have liked to drink some goat's milk for my breakfast.'

'That's no problem,' said the troll, and he took down an old flask that was high on a shelf and poured some oil from it on to the goat's head. At once the goat came to life again and was as fit as ever.

'Well that is worth knowing,' thought the youngest daughter to herself and she smiled at the troll.

As soon as he was gone she ran

into the cellar with the flask and
poured some oil on to the head of
her oldest sister who straightaway
came back to life. Oh how they

hugged each other! But then they heard the troll coming back so the eldest sister hid under a great wooden chair and the youngest sister carefully put the flask back on the shelf. She smoothed her hair and ran to greet the troll as he strode down the steep steps. She smiled warmly at him, for she was determined he would have no idea

what trickery she was up to.

Now there were only a few days left until the wedding feast. When the troll came into the youngest daughter's chamber he found her in tears again.

'Why are you crying? Have I not given you everything you could wish for and more?' he said.

'Oh yes,' she replied, 'but I wish I

had my favourite ribbon to wear on our wedding day.'

The troll said he would fetch it for her that night when the sun had set.

'If you are going that way perhaps you could take my mother some more food? She will be very grateful,' said the youngest daughter and she smiled at the troll. He still had no suspicion of her trickery.

She quickly pushed her sister in a sack and covered her head with food. The troll lifted the sack and again thought how heavy it was but he was, as we know, not very bright so he delivered the sack to the widow. Great was the rejoicing when her eldest daughter stepped out of the sack!

While the troll had been gone the youngest sister had once more

taken the flask down off the shelf
and this time restored her middle
sister to life. Oh how they hugged
each other! But then she too had to
hide quickly under the great
wooden chair when they heard the
troll returning. He found the

youngest sister in tears at the foot
of the steep stairs. There were now
only a few hours left until the
wedding feast.

'Why are you crying? Have I not
given you everything you could
wish for and more?' he asked.

'Oh yes,' she replied, 'but I do so wish to have some roses in my hair on our wedding day that come from my own garden. They have a very sweet perfume,' and she smiled at the troll.

He still had no idea how she was planning to trick him so he stumped off to the stairs, promising to go and pick the roses from her garden.

'Do take this sack to carry them in,' she said. 'I would hate them to be crushed as you carry them.'

And she gave him the sack with her middle sister hidden inside. The troll lifted the sack and again thought how heavy it was for an empty sack but he was, as we know, not very bright so he carried the sack all the way to the old widow. The troll was very tired from carrying the sack, and rather grumpy, so when the widow

offered him a cool drink in her
kitchen he accepted with alacrity.
As soon as he was out of sight, the
middle sister wriggled out of the
sack and hid under her bed until
the troll had gone, carrying the
sack now full of roses. The widow

and the eldest sister were
overjoyed to see the middle sister.

'Now we just have to wait to see
how our clever sister will escape
from the troll herself!'

Little did they know that their
clever sister had already climbed
up the steep stairs from the troll's
lair and was hidden in the trees,
awaiting his return. He climbed
down into the earth under the
mountain and called out to the
youngest sister,

'Here, I have brought your roses.
Now we can be married!'

But, of course, there was no reply.
The troll searched through all his

fine rooms but the youngest sister was nowhere to be seen. With a bellow of rage, he started to climb the stairs realising too late that his bride must have escaped. As he reached the top of the stairs, he heard her calling to him from some

way off. He ran to where he
thought her voice had come from,
only to hear her calling from
behind him. He turned back down
the path but there was her voice
coming from inside the wood
again. The youngest sister led him

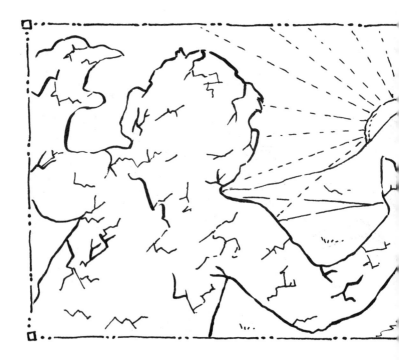

a merry dance all through the night
and he was so cross that he didn't
realise that dawn was creeping
over the mountain till with a great
cry he was turned to stone as the
first rays of the sun touched him.

The youngest sister ran home to

her mother and her sisters and they all lived happily ever after, untroubled by trolls. And what about the hen who had caused all the adventures in the first place, you may ask? To be sure the spoiled creature had only gone to the next house where she thought the food might be better!